Silly billy

pool fool

Other 🌀 bang on the door ™© titles available:

For younger readers

silly billy – time out
drama queen – puppy love
drama queen – stage struck

For older readers

friends
friends united
friends again

bang on the door™ ©

Silly billy

pool fool

First published in 2003 in Great Britain
by HarperCollins*Publishers* Ltd.

1 3 5 7 9 8 6 4 2

ISBN: 0-00-715215-9

A CIP catalogue record for this title
is available from the British Library.

Printed and bound in Great Britain by Clays Ltd, St Ives plc.

CHAPTER ONE

It was half past three and all was quiet at Number Six Fool Green, Sunnyvale. Daisy Billy was playing with her toys. Mrs Billy was putting her feet up. She'd had a hard day

working at Sunnyvale Health Centre.
Hedgehog the dog was fast asleep,
dreaming of bones. Baz the rabbit
was munching dandelion leaves.

Suddenly the peace was shattered.
BANG! CRASH! WALLOP!

The back door flew open and in came Silly Billy, at high speed. His feet were flying and his arms were whirring.

"SWOOSH!" said Silly Billy. "I'm home!"

Mr Billy followed close behind. He was the caretaker at Silly Billy's school, so they came home together.

"Silly Billy has some news," said Mr Billy wearily.

"Guess what, everyone!" said Silly Billy, opening and closing his mouth like a fish.

"What?" said Mrs Billy and Daisy,
who were sitting on the sofa.

Silly Billy put his cap back to front. He made goggles round his eyes with his fingers. Mrs Billy and Daisy looked blank.

"I'm going swimming tomorrow, with my class," said Silly Billy.

"That will be fun," Mrs Billy said enthusiastically. But then she remembered the last time Silly Billy went to the swimming pool. It hadn't been a success.

"You'll be brilliant at it, Silly Billy,"
said Daisy. She thought everything
her brother did was brilliant.

"Well, I LOVE swimming," said Silly
Billy.

Actually, Silly Billy loved paddling in the sea.

Silly Billy QUITE loved being chased by the waves.

And he really did love cooling off in the water – on very hot days only. When the water wasn't too cold.

And when it was too cold, Silly Billy liked to wrap a towel round his waist and pretend to be an Egyptian.

What Silly Billy DIDN'T love was lots of cold water. He was just a little bit scared of it.

He couldn't swim either, but somehow he'd forgotten that.

CHAPTER TWO

Silly Billy started to pack his
swimming bag straight away. First
he found a beach towel in the airing
cupboard. Then he found his favourite
swimming shorts in the drawer.

But where were the flippers? And the snorkel? The rubber ring and the mask?

toy box

Silly Billy emptied his drawers and his wardrobe. He looked in the toy box. Nothing.

"Try the garden shed," suggested Mr Billy from behind the newspaper. He soon wished he hadn't.

"Look in the cupboard under the stairs," called Mrs Billy from the sofa. She regretted it straight away.

"Didn't we put them in the loft after the summer holidays?" asked Daisy.

"I'LL go and look, said Mr and Mrs Billy together.

Mr Billy climbed the ladder up to the loft. There were boxes everywhere. One was marked *HOLIDAY GEAR*.

"This is the one," said Mr Billy, and passed it down to Mrs Billy. She gave it to Silly Billy.

holiday gear

"Cool!" said Silly Billy and opened it
right there at the foot of the ladder.

He found the flippers, the snorkel,
the mask, the rubber ring, some old
seashells and . . .

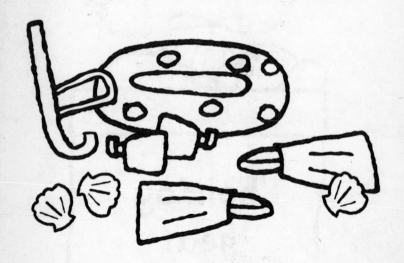

"YES!" shouted Silly Billy, "My special armbands!"

Silly Billy stuffed everything into his swimming bag except for his special armbands and the mask. He wore them to tea . . .

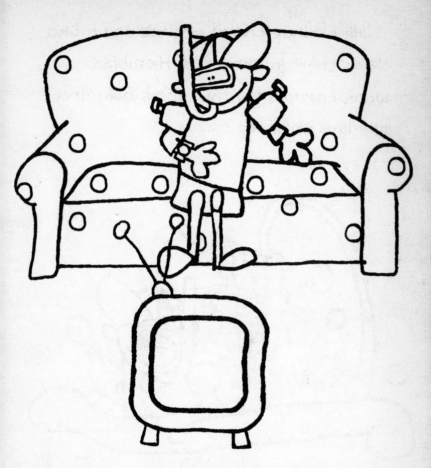

It was quite hard to watch TV in the mask, and all the air went out of the armbands but Silly Billy was far too excited to care.

He blew up the armbands again and wore them in the bath. He would have worn them in bed, but Mrs Billy drew the line at that.

CHAPTER THREE

The next morning Silly Billy was
ready for school half an hour early.
He wore his swimming trunks over his
trousers just so he couldn't possibly
leave them behind.

He blew up his armbands and wore them over his jacket.

"You look cool, Silly Billy," said Daisy.

"Hmm," said Mrs Billy. "I think the trunks look a bit silly, Silly Billy. Why don't you wear them UNDER your trousers instead?"

When Silly Billy had changed his clothes around he still had enough time to feed the rabbit.

"I'm going swimming, Baz," said Silly Billy, feeding him a lettuce leaf.

Baz chewed his leaf in silence.

"I'm going swimming, Hedgehog,"
said Silly Billy to the dog.

Hedgehog lay on his back and
paddled his legs.

"Soon I'll be able to swim as well as
you can."

"Woof!" said Hedgehog.

"Time to go, Silly Billy," called Mr Billy. "Don't forget your swimming bag!"

Off they went at last.

CHAPTER FOUR

At school Miss Sweet's class formed a long crocodile to walk to the swimming pool. Miss Sweet couldn't persuade Silly Billy to take his armbands off.

One look at Silly Billy and all the passers-by knew where the children were heading.

When they reached the swimming pool Silly Billy was first into the changing rooms . . .

And first out.

He was prepared for ANYTHING in his snorkel, his flippers and a rubber ring, which was a good thing, because he couldn't see very well through the mask, and the flippers made it hard to walk.

SPLASH!

splash

Silly Billy tumbled into the shallow end. Luckily, the rubber ring kept him afloat but Silly Billy had already decided that the water was far too COLD!

"BRRR!" he shouted, jumping up and down. "Help! It's freezing!"

Miss Sweet and the swimming instructor helped Silly Billy climb out of the water.

"You're here to learn how to swim, Silly Billy," said Miss Sweet.

But Silly Billy didn't hear her. He was peering through his mask at his friends. Some of them knew how to swim already!

Miss Sweet knocked on the mask.
"Knock, knock!" she said.
Silly Billy jumped.

knock
knock

"Take this off, Silly Billy," said Miss Sweet kindly, helping him with the snorkel. "And the flippers. And the rubber ring."

"Here's a float," said the instructor.
"In you get."

Silly Billy went down the ladder into the water and stood shivering in line with his friends.

"Now, hold your floats out in front of you and kick your legs hard!" called the instructor.

"But I CAN'T swim," Silly Billy said to himself. So he walked instead. Silly Billy walked to the side six times before Miss Sweet noticed.

"Silly Silly Billy!" said Miss Sweet. "That's not swimming! You have to take your feet off the bottom. Go on, kick!"

So Silly Billy kicked.

"Ouch!" said Drama Queen, as Silly Billy's foot caught on her leg. She kicked him back.

"Not like that, Silly Billy," she said crossly. "Like this!" and she swam off with her float.

"Now try the same thing on your backs!" said the instructor. "Hold your floats on your chests."

Silly Billy remembered to kick his legs this time. It was no use, though. He just went round and round in little circles. Poor old Silly Billy.

"I'll NEVER learn to swim," he thought sadly.

Silly Billy watched Drama Queen paddling across the pool — why couldn't he swim like that?

Miss Sweet watched Silly Billy from the side.

"Bend your knees, Silly Billy!" she urged.

Silly Billy bent his knees.

"Hold out your float!" encouraged Miss Sweet.

Silly Billy gripped his float, but it seemed to have a mind of its own. It popped out of the water and bopped him on the chin.

"Hold it tighter, Silly Billy!" said Miss Sweet. "Now, lean forwards and take your feet off the bottom."

But Silly Billy couldn't concentrate on so many things at once. He leaned forwards – and let go of the float.

And then his head went under the water.

SPLOOSH!

Silly Billy was so surprised, he forgot to shut his eyes.

He looked around under water. He could see everyone's watery arms and legs and bottoms.

And lots of bubbles.

"Cool!" thought Silly Billy. Then he ran out of breath.

SPLUTTER! SPLUTTER!

Silly Silly Billy!

Silly Billy's feet hit the bottom and he shot up as fast as he could.

He scrabbled towards the steps and Miss Sweet helped him out.

Silly Billy coughed and spluttered.

cough

splutter

"I CAN'T SWIM!" he howled in despair when he'd finished coughing.

"Not without my special armbands, anyway."

"How about trying to swim on your back again, Silly Billy?" said Miss Sweet.

"You might find it easier this time."

"No I wouldn't," said Silly Billy.

"But you'd like a badge, wouldn't you?" asked his teacher.

no. 1 swimmer

"Oh, all right," said Silly Billy. "I'll try to swim on my back. At least my face won't go under water." And he bravely went back down the steps.

"Here goes," thought Silly Billy.

"Hold your floats on your chests," said the instructor.

Silly Billy put his float on his chest and remembered to kick his legs this time.

It was no use, though. He just went round and round in little circles — AGAIN! Poor Silly Billy.

"I'll never, EVER learn to swim," he thought sadly. "And I'll never ever get a badge."

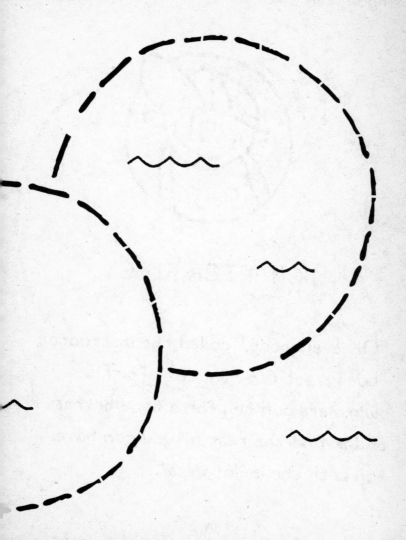

CHAPTER FIVE

"OK everybody," called the instructor.
"We've got ten minutes left. The
swimmers can try for a ten-metres
badge, and the rest of you can have
fun with the inflatables."

He pointed to the side of the pool nearest the changing rooms for the swimmers and the side furthest from the changing rooms for everyone else.

Silly Billy looked at the inflatables.
There were rubber rings and
colourful rubber balls. There was an
inflatable shark and even some
armbands. But they weren't half as
good as his SPECIAL armbands.

"I left my special armbands in the changing rooms. Can I fetch them?" Silly Billy asked Miss Sweet.

"I suppose so," she replied. "There isn't much time, so you'll have to hurry."

Silly Billy grabbed his special armbands and slid them on to his arms as he hurried back to the pool.

Did Silly Billy walk round to the far side of the pool where the inflatables were?

No, there wasn't time. He jumped straight into the water by the changing rooms. His trusty armbands would keep him afloat.

He jumped straight into the other swimmers.

Silly Billy pretended he was one of them as he made his way to the far side.

"I quite like being in the water now I've got my armbands on," he thought.

He swam alongside Drama Queen.
"Swimming's much easier with armbands than with a float," he said.

"Go away," snapped Drama Queen.
"You're distracting me."

"Just passing through," said Silly Billy.

"Well, you're in the wrong place," said Drama Queen.

"Miss Sweet!" she called. "Silly
Billy's on the wrong side of the pool."
But Silly Billy was enjoying himself.
He was pretending to be Hedgehog
swimming doggy paddle. He waved
at Miss Sweet from the water.

Miss Sweet waved back. She'd
noticed something about Silly Billy's
special armbands.

"Keep going, Silly Billy!" she shouted.

"All right!" Silly Billy shouted back.

Silly Billy ploughed on through the children who were playing with the water toys.

When he reached the other side, Miss Sweet told him to get out of the water.

"Uh-oh," thought Silly Billy. "I'm in trouble."

"I didn't mean to get in the way of the real swimmers," he explained to her. "I just wanted to get across to the other side of the pool."

"Oh, SILLY Silly Billy," said
Miss Sweet. "You ARE a real swimmer!"
   Silly Billy was puzzled.
   "Look at your armbands," said
Miss Sweet.

Silly Billy looked at them. They
looked smaller than before.

"They've gone down," Miss Sweet
said. "There's no air in them. The
armbands weren't keeping you afloat,
Silly Billy – YOU were!"

"Me? Swimming?" asked Silly Billy.
"Of course!" said Miss Sweet. "And
you've earned yourself a badge!"

"I CAN SWIM!" yelled Silly Billy and jumped in the water again. "Didn't I say I loved swimming?"

CHAPTER SIX

Back in the changing rooms there
was one little problem. Remember
how Silly Billy had put his swimming
shorts on UNDER his trousers?
He'd packed everything he needed

into his swimming bag EXCEPT . . .

Well, you can guess.

"Oh dear. No dry underpants," thought Silly Billy. "Never mind, I'll soon dry off." And he put his trousers on over his wet shorts.

Miss Sweet's class formed a long
crocodile to walk back to school.

When they arrived at Sunnyvale Primary it was time for lunch. Silly Billy hung up his things and stood in the queue.

Soon the other children noticed a little trail of drips where Silly Billy had been. Silly Billy sat down with his friends.

A small puddle started to form
around his feet. Some children
started to point and giggle.

Luckily Miss Sweet came to the rescue. "Silly Silly Billy!" she said, laughing. "You've brought some of the swimming pool back to school with you! Come with me and we'll find you some dry clothes."

At half past three, all was quiet at Number Six Fool Green. Until . . .

CRASH! BANG! WALLOP!

In came Silly Billy. "Guess what, everyone!" he said, dumping his swimming bag on the floor.

"What?" asked Mrs Billy and Daisy Billy.

"I can SWIM!" said Silly Billy.
"And I've got a badge to prove it."
"There, I told you so," said Daisy,
"I knew you'd be brilliant."

pool fool

The characters in this book were
played by:

Silly Billy	himself
Mr Billy	'handyman'
Mrs Billy	'mum'
Daisy Billy	'fun in the sun'
Miss Sweet	'lovely'
School Kids	'friends'
Swim Instructor	'footballer'
Drama Queen	herself
Hedgehog	'puppy'
Baz	'rabbit'

bang on the door™©

Silly billy
**Follow the adventures of Silly Billy —
the silliest boy in the WHOLE world.**

TIME OUT

Silly Billy has a brand new watch . . .
But he doesn't quite know how to use it.
When its alarm goes off one hour early
Silly Billy decides to get HIMSELF
ready for school. And that's when the
trouble starts . . .

Collins

An imprint of HarperCollinsPublishers

bang on the door™ ©

drama queen

Drama Queen makes a drama out of
EVERYTHING. Read about her
latest adventure in . . .

PUPPY LOVE

Drama Queen knows EXACTLY what
she wants, a sweet, cuddly puppy all of her
very own. But her mum and dad are
not impressed! Then her nanny Leo has
an idea . . . But will it put Drama Queen
off dogs for ever?

Collins

▪ *An imprint of HarperCollinsPublishers*

bang on the door™©

drama queen

Drama Queen makes a drama out of
EVERYTHING. Read about her
latest adventure in . . .

STAGE STRUCK

Drama Queen is very excited!
She loves to dance and sing and act
and she is desperate to be Snow White
in the school play.
But will she get the part?
And who will play Prince Charming?

Collins
An imprint of HarperCollins*Publishers*

⊙ bang on the door™©

friends

Together we make things happen!

Meet Spex, Jude, Tiger, Sugar, Spice, Flash and Cookie. Follow their adventures as they set up a newspaper and report on crimes, local issues and Tiger's mum's cooking!

FRIENDS

The Friends set up the *Sunnyvale Standard* to fight the plans of a dastardly property developer.

FRIENDS UNITED

Disaster! The local pool has been closed down —and just before the summer hols! It's a race against time as the Friends swing into action to save their pool.

Collins

An imprint of HarperCollins*Publishers*

bang on the door ™ ©

poo jokebook
Every pun is guaranteed to pong in this stinky collection!

What do you get if you cross an elephant with a bottle of laxative?
Out of the way!

What do you get if you eat baked beans and onions?
Tear gas!

Packed with wicked whiffs, real stinkers and nasty niffs – jokes that will run and run!

Collins

🏠 *An imprint of HarperCollinsPublishers*

⊙bang on the door™©

Collect 5 tokens and get a free poster!*

All you have to do is collect five funky tokens!
You can snip one from any of these cool Bang on the Door books!

0 00 715209 4

0 00 715309 0

0 00 715212 4

0 00 715210 8

Send 5 tokens with a completed coupon to: Bang on the Door Poster Offer

PO Box 142, Horsham, RH13 5FJ (UK residents)

c/- HarperCollins Publishers (NZ) Ltd,
PO Box 1, Auckland (NZ residents)

c/- HarperCollins Publishers, PO Box 321,
Pymble NSW 2073, Australia
(for Australian residents)

0 00 715220 5

First name: .... Surname: ....

Address: ....

....

....

Postcode: .... Child's date of birth: .... / .... / ....

email address: ....

Signature of parent/guardian: ....

Tick here if you do not wish to receive further information about children's books ☐

SB 2 / token

Terms and Conditions: Proof of sending cannot be considered proof of receipt.

Not redeemable for cash. Please allow 28 days for delivery. Photocopied tokens not accepted.

Offer open to UK, New Zealand and Australia only while stocks last.*rrp £3.99